Help!

ALL ABOUT TELLING TIME

Written by Kirsten Hall

Illustrated by Bev Luedecke

children's press®

A Division of Scholastic Inc.
New York Toronto London Auckland Sydney
Mexico City New Delhi Hong Kong
Danbury, Connecticut

About the Author

Kirsten Hall, formerly an early-childhood teacher,
is a children's book editor in New York City. She has been
writing books for children since she was thirteen years old
and now has over sixty titles in print.

About the Illustrator

Bev Luedecke enjoys life and nature in Colorado.
Her sparkling personality and artistic flair are reflected in her
creation of Beastieville, a world filled with lovable Beasties
that are sure to delight children of all ages.

Library of Congress Cataloging-in-Publication Data

Hall, Kirsten.
  Help! : all about telling time / written by Kirsten Hall ; illustrated
by Bev Luedecke.
      p. cm.
Summary: When Pooky runs out of time to pick enough berries for her
Beastie Berry pies, her friends pitch in to help.
  ISBN 0-516-22890-0 (lib. bdg.)   0-516-24655-0 (pbk.)
  [1. Helpfulness–Fiction. 2. Friendship–Fiction. 3. Pies–Fiction. 4.
Stories in rhyme.] I. Luedecke, Bev, ill. II. Title.
  PZ8.3.H146He 2003
  [E]–dc21
                              2003001585

1 2 3 4 5 6 7 8 9 10 R 12 11 10 09 08 07 06 05 04 03

A NOTE TO PARENTS AND TEACHERS

Welcome to the world of the Beasties, where learning is FUN. In each of the charming stories in this series, the Beasties deal with character issues that every child can identify with. Each story reinforces appropriate concept skills for kindergartners and first graders, while simultaneously encouraging problem-solving skills. Following are just a few of the ways that you can help children get the most from this delightful series.

Stories to be read and enjoyed

Encourage children to read the stories aloud. The rhyming verses make them fun to read. Then ask them to think about alternate solutions to some of the problems that the Beasties have faced or to imagine alternative endings. Invite children to think about what they would have done if they were in the story and to recall similar things that have happened to them.

Activities reinforce the learning experience

The activities at the end of the books offer a way for children to put their new skills to work. They complement the story and are designed to help children develop specific skills and build confidence. Use these activities to reinforce skills. But don't stop there. Encourage children to find ways to build on these skills during the course of the day.

Learning opportunities are everywhere

Use this book as a starting point for talking about how we use reading skills or math or social studies concepts in everyday life. When we search for a phone number in the telephone book and scan names in alphabetical order or check a list, we are using reading skills. When we keep score at a baseball game or divide a class into even numbered teams, we are using math.

The more you can help children see that the skills they are learning in school really do have a place in everyday life, the more they will think of learning as something that is part of their lives, not as a chore to be borne. Plus you will be sending the important message that learning is fun.

Madeline Boskey Olsen, Ph.D.
Developmental Psychologist

Bee-Bop

Puddles

Slider

Wilbur

Pip & Zip

Flippet

Pooky

Mr. Rigby

Smudge

We're the Beasties

Toggles

It is such a sunny day.
Pooky looks up at her clock.

What time is it? The clock says ten.
It is time to take a walk.

Pooky loves to take long walks.
She walks to the big oak tree.

She sees something hanging there.
"What is that? What could it be?"

"I think Toggles painted this.
There will be a Beastie Fair!

There will be a fair really soon!
I must bake something to share!"

"I will bake my berry pies!
There is so much I must do!

I must get some eggs and milk.
I must go get berries, too!"

Pooky finds the berry patch.
"Wow! These berries sure look great!"

She picks berries all day long.
It is starting to get late!

"How did it get late so fast?
I still need so many more!

How will I get all I need?
My clock shows that it is four!"

"Hi there, Pooky!" It is Smudge.
"You have lots to do. Oh, dear!

You look like you need a friend.
It is good that I am here!"

"Hi there, Bee-Bop! You will help?
Zip and Pip, you will help too?

Smudge is working very hard.
There is lots for us to do!"

Slider slides up to his friends.
"It looks like you need a tail!"

Puddles sees her friends outside.
"I will help. Give me a pail!"

Wilbur has not come to help.
"We need you to help us, too!"

"Fine," says Wilbur. "I will help.
Tell me what I have to do."

Pooky looks at him and smiles.
"I think we are done at last.

Thank you all for helping me.
We picked these berries very fast!"

Pooky bakes pies all night long.
Berry pies are everywhere.

"I need help again, my friends!
Help me get these to the Fair!"

COUNTING TIME

1. What time is it on Pooky's clock when she goes for her walk?

2. What time is it on Pooky's watch when Zip, Pip, and Bee-Bop come to help?

SOUNDS LIKE...

The word "slime" sounds a lot like "time". What are some other words that sound like "time"?

LET'S TALK ABOUT IT

Pooky is lucky she has friends who want to help her.

1. Who are some people who have helped you when you needed it?

2. When and how have you helped other people?

3. What does it feel like when someone wants to help you?

4. Why is helping such a nice thing?

WORD LIST

a	finds	last	Pip	thank
again	fine	late	Pooky	that
all	for	like	Puddles	the
am	four	long	really	there
and	friend	look	says	these
are	friends	looks	sees	think
at	get	lots	share	this
bake	give	loves	she	to
bakes	go	many	shows	too
be	good	me	Slider	Toggles
Beastie	great	milk	slides	time
Bee-Bop	hanging	more	smiles	tree
berry	hard	much	Smudge	up
berries	has	must	so	us
big	have	my	some	very
clock	help	need	something	walk
come	helping	night	soon	walks
could	her	not	starting	we
day	here	oak	still	what
did	hi	outside	such	Wilbur
do	him	pail	sunny	will
done	his	painted	sure	working
eggs	how	patch	tail	wow
everywhere	I	picked	take	you
fair	is	picks	tell	Zip
fast	it	pies	ten	